Sophie's Wheels

by Debora Pearson
art by Nora Hilb

annick press

Toronto • New York • Vancouver

We acknowledge the support of the Canada Council for the Arts, the Ontario Arts Council, and
the Government of Canada through the Book Publishing Industry Development Program
(BPIDP) for our publishing activities.

Cataloging in Publication

Pearson, Debora
    Sophie's wheels / by Debora Pearson ; art by Nora Hilb.

ISBN-13: 978-1-55451-038-2 (bound)
ISBN-10: 1-55451-038-4 (bound)
ISBN-13: 978-1-55451-037-5 (pbk.)
ISBN-10: 1-55451-037-6 (pbk.)

    I. Hilb, Nora II. Title.

PS8581.E383S66 2006   jC813'.6   C2006-901035-8

The art in this book was rendered in watercolor.
The text was typeset in Galahad.

Distributed in Canada by: Published in the U.S.A. by:
Firefly Books Ltd.   Annick Press (U.S.) Ltd.
66 Leek Crescent   Distributed in the U.S.A. by:
Richmond Hill, ON   Firefly Books (U.S.) Inc.
L4B 1H1   P.O. Box 1338
                                 Ellicott Station
                                 Buffalo, NY 14205

Printed in China.

Visit us at: www.annickpress.com

This story is for Nora Hilb, with
affection and appreciation.
—D.P.

To my dear friend Graciela R.
—N.H.

When Sophie was small
She rode on wheels
Bouncy baby buggy wheels

Boing-ity, boing-ity
Squeak, squeak
She rocked and rocked
And fell asleep

The world rolled by
The world peeked in

Sophie sat up
Smiled at everything!

Hustle bustle
Down the sidewalk
Here comes Sophie
In her stroller

Legs stand close
While grown-ups chat

Hello bugs!

Hello cat!

Squoosh! Scrunch!
Sophie's stuck
Sometimes wheels
Won't go in snow

Zippy sled
Slip-slides ahead

Wheels to push

Wheels to pull

Screeching, grinding ...

Whooshing home

Beep! Beep! **BLAP!**
Traffic jam
Trucks and cars
Are v-e-r-y slow

Sophie's wagon
Rattles past them
Faster, Sophie, faster!

Two wheels

Three wheels

Now Sophie has four
(Two big ones, two small ones)
Where will she go?

Tring! Tring!

The world rolls by
She's on her own

Around the corner ...

And Sophie's home!